# My Christmas Safari

Fran Manushkin / *pictures by* R.W. Alley

**Dial Books for Young Readers**  New York

*This book is for my African safari friends—*
*especially Becky Serens and Marcia Hostetler*  F. M.

*For Katy and Dale, world travelers,*
*and for Barbara, lover of the wildebeest*  R. W. A.

Published by Dial Books for Young Readers
A Division of Penguin Books USA Inc./375 Hudson Street/New York, New York 10014

Text copyright © 1993 by Fran Manushkin/Pictures copyright © 1993 by R. W. Alley
All rights reserved/Design by Nancy R. Leo
Printed in Hong Kong by South China Printing Company (1988) Limited
First Edition/10 9 8 7 6 5 4 3 2 1

Library of Congress Cataloging in Publication Data
Manushkin, Fran.
My Christmas safari / Fran Manushkin : pictures by R. W. Alley.—1st ed.   p.  cm.
*Summary:* A cumulative counting song describes the animals seen on an imaginative photo safari
to Africa. Includes music to set the words to the melody of "The Twelve Days of Christmas."
ISBN 0-8037-1294-4.—ISBN 0-8037-1295-2 (lib. bdg.)
[1. Animals—Songs and music.  2. Counting.  3. Songs.]  I. Alley, R. W. (Robert W.), ill.  II. Title.
PZ8.3.M3565My  1993  [E]—dc20  92-28643  CIP  AC

*The full-color artwork was prepared using watercolors with an ink pen line.*

On the first day of Christmas
my father showed to me:
    A green truck for our safari.

On the second day of Christmas
my father showed to me:
   Two leopard cubs
   and a green truck for our safari.

On the third day of Christmas
my father showed to me:
   Three wildebeests,
   Two leopard cubs,
   and a green truck for our safari.

On the fourth day of Christmas
my father showed to me:
    Four shy giraffes,
    Three wildebeests,
    Two leopard cubs,
    and a green truck for our safari.

On the fifth day of Christmas
my father showed to me:
   Five big baboons!
   Four shy giraffes,
   Three wildebeests,
   Two leopard cubs,
   and a green truck for our safari.

On the sixth day of Christmas
my father showed to me:
   Six zebras barking,
   Five big baboons!
   Four shy giraffes,
   Three wildebeests,
   Two leopard cubs,
   and a green truck for our safari.

On the seventh day of Christmas
my father showed to me:
   Seven flamingos flying,
   Six zebras barking,
   Five big baboons!
   Four shy giraffes,
   Three wildebeests,
   Two leopard cubs,
   and a green truck for our safari.

On the eighth day of Christmas
my father showed to me:
    Eight hippos yawning,
    Seven flamingos flying,
    Six zebras barking,
    Five big baboons!
    Four shy giraffes,
    Three wildebeests,
    Two leopard cubs,
    and a green truck for our safari.

On the ninth day of Christmas
my father showed to me:
    Nine hyenas howling,
    Eight hippos yawning,
    Seven flamingos flying,
    Six zebras barking,
    Five big baboons!
    Four shy giraffes,
    Three wildebeests,
    Two leopard cubs,
    and a green truck for our safari.

On the tenth day of Christmas
my father showed to me:
　　Ten topis trotting,
　　Nine hyenas howling,
　　Eight hippos yawning,
　　Seven flamingos flying,
　　Six zebras barking,
　　Five big baboons!
　　Four shy giraffes,
　　Three wildebeests,
　　Two leopard cubs,
　　and a green truck for our safari.

On the eleventh day of Christmas
my father showed to me:
Eleven lions roaring,
Ten topis trotting,
Nine hyenas howling,
Eight hippos yawning,
Seven flamingos flying,
Six zebras barking,
Five big baboons!
Four shy giraffes,
Three wildebeests,
Two leopard cubs,
and a green truck for our safari.

On the twelfth day of Christmas
my father showed to me:
  Twelve elephants trumpeting,
  Eleven lions roaring…

Ten topis trotting,
Nine hyenas howling,
Eight hippos yawning,
Seven flamingos flying,
Six zebras barking,
Five big baboons…

Four shy giraffes,
Three wildebeests,
Two leopard cubs—
and a green truck for our safari!